From me
to You

First published in 2003 in Great Britain by Gullane Children's Books
This paperback edition published in 2004 by

Gullane Children's Books
an imprint of Pinwheel Limited
Winchester House, 259-269 Old Marylebone Road,
London NW1 5XJ

1 3 5 7 9 10 8 6 4 2

Text © Anthony France 2003
Illustrations © Tiphanie Beeke 2003

The right of Anthony France and Tiphanie Beeke to be identified as the author and illustrator of this work
has been asserted by them in accordance with the Copyright, Designs, and Patents Act, 1988.
A CIP record for this title is available from the British Library.

ISBN 1-86233-333-5 hardback
ISBN 1-86233-504-4 paperback

Printed and bound in China

From Me to You

Anthony France • Tiphanie Beeke

GULLANE
CHILDREN'S BOOKS

Although a happy morning
was struggling to find
a way into his bedroom,
Rat was feeling miserable.
Not wanting to get up
or stay in bed, he could
feel another case of
the dressing-gown blues
coming on.

Dressing-gown blues is when you don't
wash your face or comb your whiskers, and just
mope around all day long in your dressing-gown.
Rat was good at this, as he did it every day.

He crawled out of bed into his
dressing-gown and slunk downstairs.

For breakfast Rat had half a spoonful of condensed milk and a cold cup of yesterday's leftover tea.

"It's not just that I've nothing to do," he thought, "I've no one to do it with. My friends never call round these days, and doing nothing with no one is no fun at all."

It was while Rat was sighing a very sad sigh indeed that he heard his letterbox clank. When Rat went to look, he discovered a cheerful yellow envelope.

Rat opened it and read:

Dear Rat
This letter is from someone who really admires you and is glad of your friendship. It comes from me. I think you are very special, and I just want you to know how lucky I feel to have such a true and dear friend as you.

All my love...

But there was no name at the bottom.

Rat read the letter again. And then, just to make sure, he read it another ten times.

"How wonderful!" said Rat. "But I haven't a clue who sent it . . . unless . . . why, of course, it must be from Mouse! How very kind of him. I'll go and thank him right away."

He shot upstairs,
threw off his dressing-gown,

pulled on some clothes,

washed his face,

brushed his teeth,

combed his whiskers

and skipped out into the morning, clutching his letter.

"It's a lovely letter," said Mouse, who was delighted to see Rat, "but since the storm I've had little time to write to my friends. I've been busy repairing my roof."

It was the first that Rat had heard about Mouse's damaged roof, and for the rest of the day all else was forgotten as they worked together to mend it.

It was only when they had finished that Mouse casually
wondered aloud who could have sent the letter.

"Beats me!" grinned Rat, who felt happy just thinking about it.

"But I'll find out tomorrow."

The next morning, Rat was dunked, dressed and downstairs before dawn.
He made a fresh pot of tea and had two extra spoonfuls of condensed milk.
The sun was rising over the fields when Rat stepped out of his house
and set off along the river. He was now almost certain that the someone
who loved him was Frog. She hadn't been to see Rat for ages.

Rat knocked at Frog's door for a long time before he heard a faint voice from inside.

"It's me," said Rat. "What's the matter?"

"Nothing much," replied Frog, "but you'll have to let yourself in."

Rat was shocked to discover Frog had a broken leg.
"I'm all right," said Frog. "It has been a bit difficult, just hopping around in circles, but lots of friends have dropped by to help."

"I'd have dropped by too, if I'd known," said Rat, guiltily chewing a whisker. "So, can I help you now?" he asked.

It was not until Rat was out shopping for Frog that he realised that he had quite forgotten to ask if she had sent the letter.

He quickly compared Frog's hand-written shopping list . . .

TOMATOES
LEEKS
RADISH
PACKET
OF OATMEAL

. . . with the words on his yellow envelope

. . . and he knew one thing for sure.
The letter had not been written by Frog.

"Wake up, daydreamer," said two voices suddenly. "What have you there that's so interesting?"

It was Rat's friends Mole and Mole and their son, Baby Mole.

"Somebody sent me this," answered Rat, "but I don't know who."

"Well, it's not from us," said the Moles. "We called on you recently, but we haven't written."

"You called?" asked Rat. "When?"

"On Wednesday afternoon," the Moles said, "but your curtains were still drawn, so we left you in peace."

Rat finished the shopping, then returned to Frog's house. He had planned to make her lunch, but Mouse had turned up with a pie.

"Any luck with your mysterious letter-writer?" asked Mouse.

Rat shook his head, though not at all sadly. And then, for the briefest of moments, he thought he saw Mouse wink at Frog.

After lunch, Rat set off once again to solve the mystery.
He felt on top of the world. He had spent so much time
wondering who it was who thought him special that he
was actually beginning to feel special.

He now decided to call on Bat.

"Who's that?" said Bat. "What do you want?"
"It's Rat, Bat," said Rat. "Hello!"
"Goodbye," said Bat. "I'm busy!"
"But it's me, your friend," pleaded Rat.
"I want to know how you are . . . and
whether you've written to me recently."

"Course not," said Bat. "No one writes to me, so I don't write to them. And if you were a real friend, you'd have called on me before now. So just push off."

Something was clearly wrong with Bat. He was lonely and unhappy – and what's more, he was still in his dressing-gown.

It was a sad and sorry Rat who got home that evening – only he was no longer sad and sorry for himself.

"Poor old Bat," he muttered. "He's down in the dumps, but what he said is right. If I'd been a real friend, I'd have visited before. The only reason I went today was to find out something for myself."

And then Rat read his precious letter for the last time.
"Finding out who wrote this just doesn't seem important any more," he thought. "Whoever sent it, I don't deserve it. I've never been a true friend to anyone. Well, tomorrow I'm going to change all that."

For Rat, tomorrow came very early the next day. He'd gone to bed
with the seed of an idea, but it soon grew into an exciting plan.
So Rat got up at three to get started.

Tomorrow came very early for Mouse too! It arrived at five, when Rat woke him up.

"I've written lots of invitations for a party and I want you and Frog to help me deliver them. What do you think of that?"

At five in the morning Mouse seldom thought much about anything, but by seven he was more excited than Rat.

"Let's fetch Frog," he said.

The three of them had great fun that day. Mouse enjoyed not
working on his roof, Frog enjoyed the fresh air, and Rat just
enjoyed being with friends. They walked for miles, and by
late afternoon all the invitations were delivered.
All, except for one.

Bat's curtains were still drawn
when they arrived at his house.
Rat quietly pushed the invitation
in the letterbox, and then pulled
out a bright red envelope
from his pocket.

"What's that?" asked Mouse.
"Just a special letter for Bat,"
whispered Rat, "that's all."
    And then, for the briefest of
moments, Mouse and Frog thought
Rat winked at them – and they
were right. He did.

Dear Bat

This letter is from someone
who really admires you and is
glad of your friendship. It
comes from me. I think you
are very special, and I just
want you to know how lucky I
feel to have such a true and
dear friend as you.

All my love